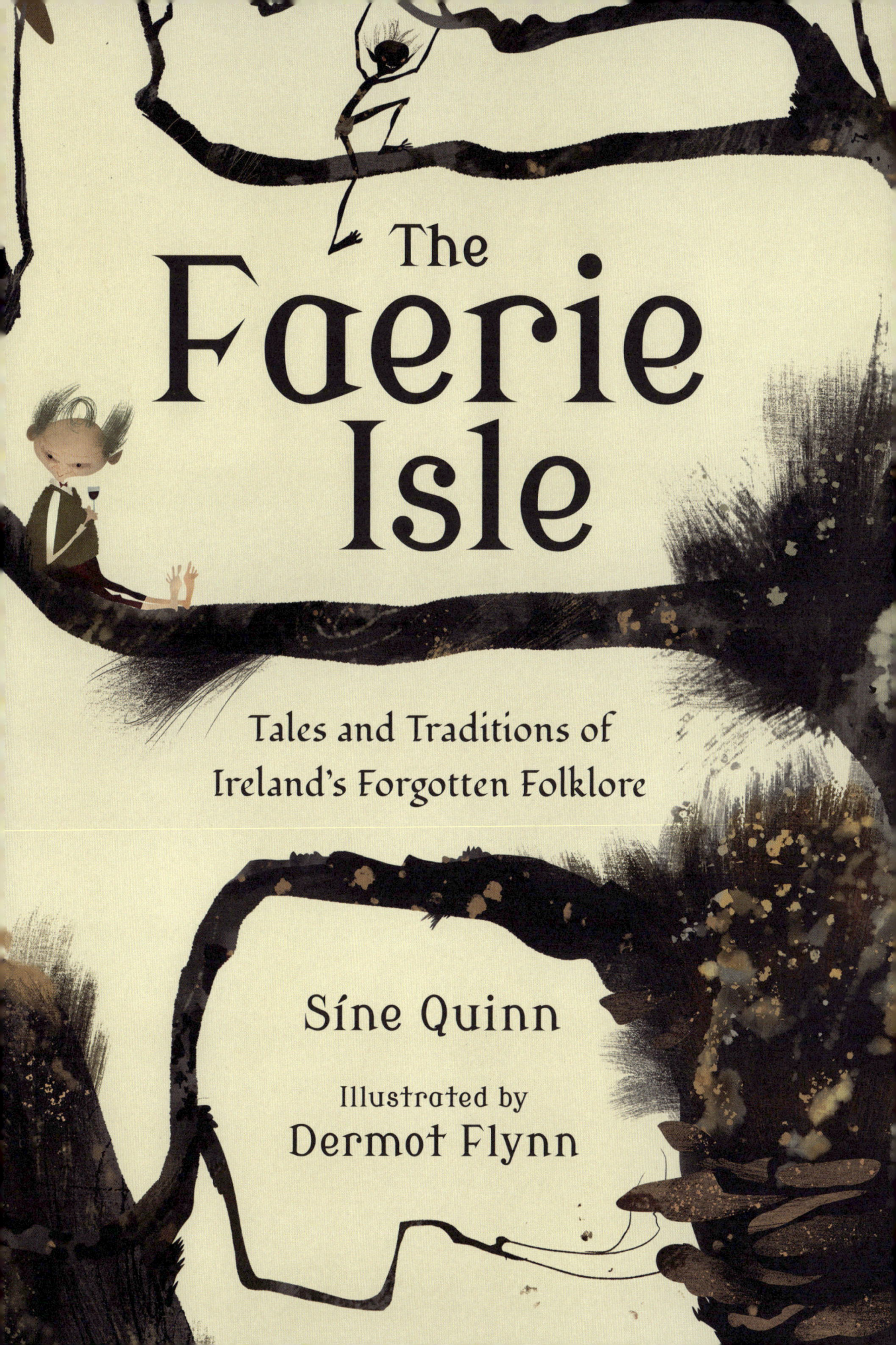

CONTENTS

Mermaid
12

Leprechaun
16

Giant
20

Banshee
24

The Good People
28

The Charmer
32

Wild Water Horse
36

Changeling
40

Faerie Cat
44

Faerie Dog
48

Selkie
52

Pooka
56

Tree Faerie
60

Headless Horseman
64

Shapeshifter
68

Sheerie
72

FOREWORD

I grew up in Galway, on the west coast of Ireland, hearing stories about faeries from an early age. One thing I learned very quickly was that our faeries are nothing like the ones you see in traditional storybooks, with their gossamer wings and magic wands. No! Irish faeries are more likely to be shapeshifters, tricksters or revenge-seeking, lesson-teaching fiends.

I've heard it said that some faeries are kindly, of course, and have been known to help us humans. I've heard they can give gifts of music and good fortune to those they like. But there are also stories of them leading unsuspecting humans astray or into the faerie realm – and only some return.

Irish people have always been wary of the faeries; wary because the faeries live beside them, among them, above and below. A stroll down a country road could take you past a faerie tree, a faerie fort, a faerie hill. Place names whisper to you of otherworldly forces: *Carraigaphooka* (the púca's rock) in Cork; *Pollaphuca* (the púca's cavern) in Wicklow; *Clochán an Phúca* (the púca's causeway) on the Aran Islands.

This, then, is a very special book – a book steeped in magic and lore. Normally, these characters and their stories come to life in dark places, on cold, wet nights when there is a heavy mist to cover all traces. These stories are usually whispered, hidden, delivered carefully and with a little shake in the voice.

For generations, Irish folklore has been passed from mouth to mouth, or, as we say in Irish, "from knee to knee!" as grandmothers, grandfathers, uncles and aunts gave back the stories they had gathered throughout their lives – one treasure at a time.

Síne Quinn and her co-conspirator, Dermot Flynn, have walked a fine line in this book. On the one hand, they speak respectfully about the "good people"; on the other, they give away many of their secrets. The illustrations, for example, are full of light; no corner is left unseen. A brave decision.

Nonetheless, I hope you enjoy reading about the wailing banshees, the lucky leprechauns and the seductive selkies, who roam throughout the pages of this book.

It is entirely up to you, but I would read this book in daylight, surrounded by your own kind. An iron nail secreted in your pocket would be a good investment. It may prevent you being carried away by the "good people". If you should end up in the faerie world, however, don't eat anything, don't drink anything and take nothing with you when you leave.

Read on, oh brave and fearless reader! (You *are* brave, aren't you?)

Travel safely!

Patricia Forde
Laureate na nÓg (2023–2026)

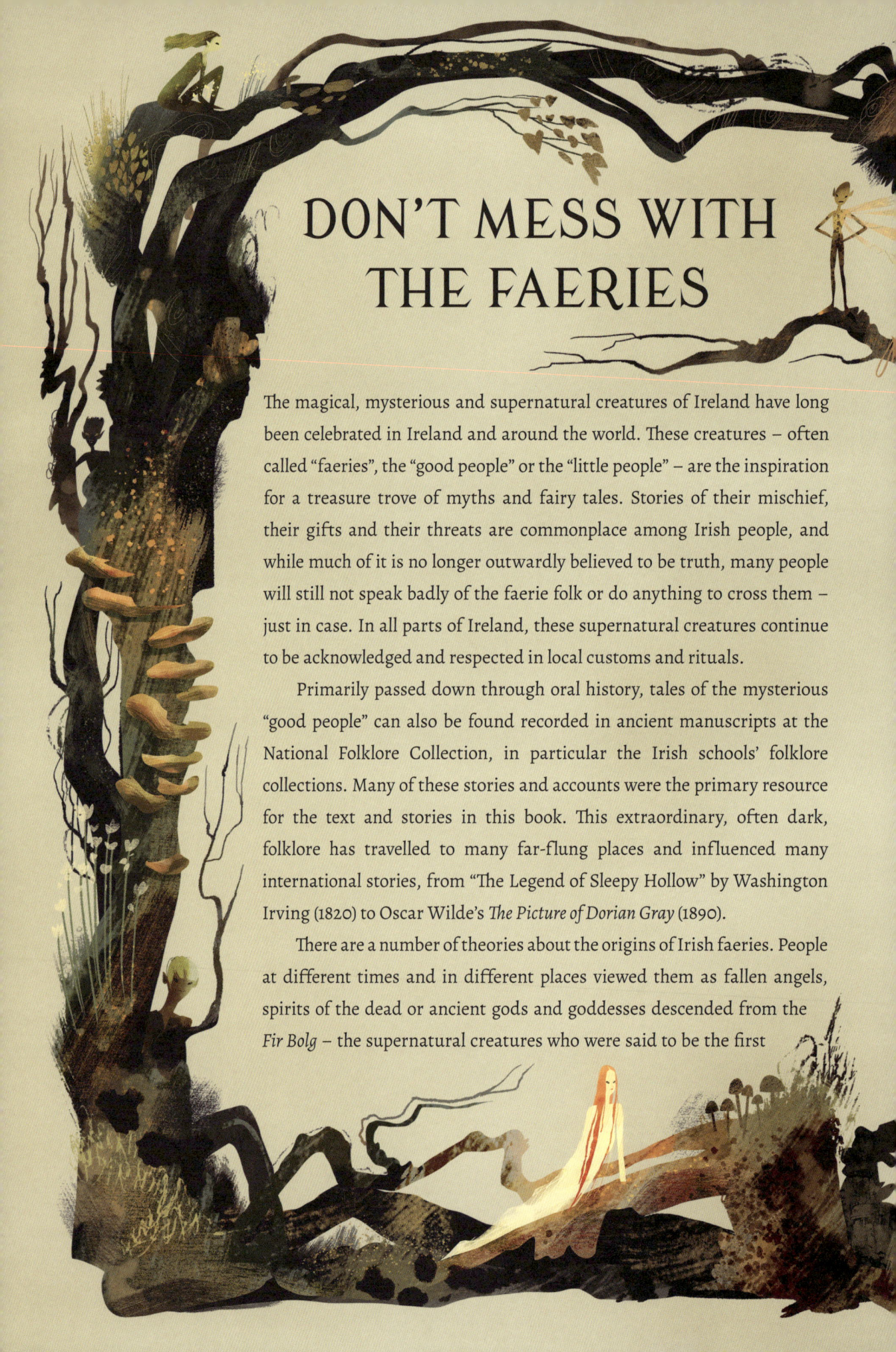

DON'T MESS WITH THE FAERIES

The magical, mysterious and supernatural creatures of Ireland have long been celebrated in Ireland and around the world. These creatures – often called "faeries", the "good people" or the "little people" – are the inspiration for a treasure trove of myths and fairy tales. Stories of their mischief, their gifts and their threats are commonplace among Irish people, and while much of it is no longer outwardly believed to be truth, many people will still not speak badly of the faerie folk or do anything to cross them – just in case. In all parts of Ireland, these supernatural creatures continue to be acknowledged and respected in local customs and rituals.

Primarily passed down through oral history, tales of the mysterious "good people" can also be found recorded in ancient manuscripts at the National Folklore Collection, in particular the Irish schools' folklore collections. Many of these stories and accounts were the primary resource for the text and stories in this book. This extraordinary, often dark, folklore has travelled to many far-flung places and influenced many international stories, from "The Legend of Sleepy Hollow" by Washington Irving (1820) to Oscar Wilde's *The Picture of Dorian Gray* (1890).

There are a number of theories about the origins of Irish faeries. People at different times and in different places viewed them as fallen angels, spirits of the dead or ancient gods and goddesses descended from the *Fir Bolg* – the supernatural creatures who were said to be the first

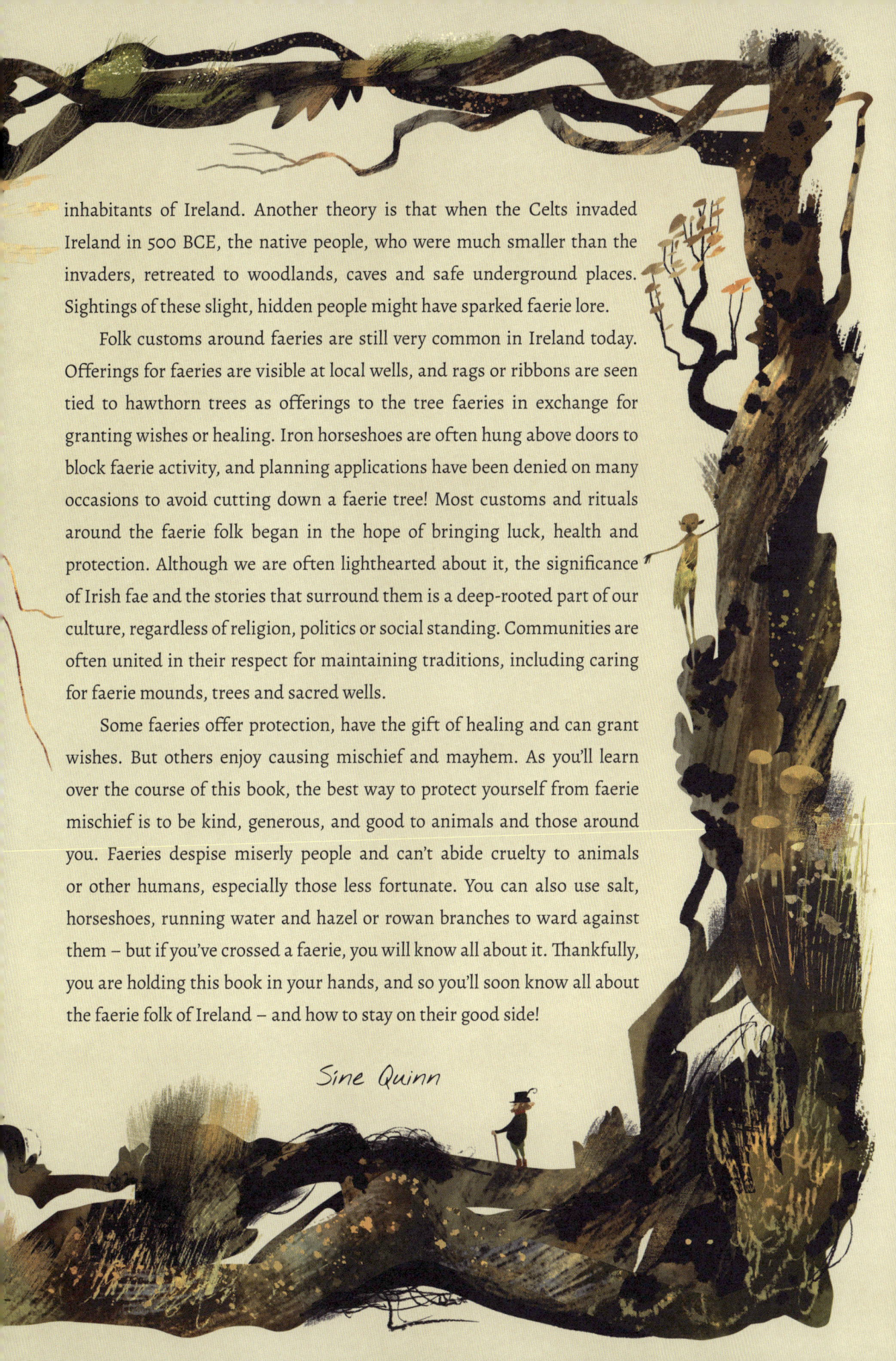

inhabitants of Ireland. Another theory is that when the Celts invaded Ireland in 500 BCE, the native people, who were much smaller than the invaders, retreated to woodlands, caves and safe underground places. Sightings of these slight, hidden people might have sparked faerie lore.

Folk customs around faeries are still very common in Ireland today. Offerings for faeries are visible at local wells, and rags or ribbons are seen tied to hawthorn trees as offerings to the tree faeries in exchange for granting wishes or healing. Iron horseshoes are often hung above doors to block faerie activity, and planning applications have been denied on many occasions to avoid cutting down a faerie tree! Most customs and rituals around the faerie folk began in the hope of bringing luck, health and protection. Although we are often lighthearted about it, the significance of Irish fae and the stories that surround them is a deep-rooted part of our culture, regardless of religion, politics or social standing. Communities are often united in their respect for maintaining traditions, including caring for faerie mounds, trees and sacred wells.

Some faeries offer protection, have the gift of healing and can grant wishes. But others enjoy causing mischief and mayhem. As you'll learn over the course of this book, the best way to protect yourself from faerie mischief is to be kind, generous, and good to animals and those around you. Faeries despise miserly people and can't abide cruelty to animals or other humans, especially those less fortunate. You can also use salt, horseshoes, running water and hazel or rowan branches to ward against them – but if you've crossed a faerie, you will know all about it. Thankfully, you are holding this book in your hands, and so you'll soon know all about the faerie folk of Ireland – and how to stay on their good side!

Sine Quinn

MERMAID
·· MAIGHDEAN MHARA ··

Mermaids have been depicted in art and literature for many hundreds of years. The first image of a merman was found in a Phoenician carving from 700 BCE, almost three thousand years ago! Medieval Irish manuscripts contain many accounts of these beautiful creatures, often spotted along the coast or in the waters of Lough Neagh.

Mermaids are often regarded as messengers, sometimes of good tidings but also of misfortune and even death, and it is thought to be unlucky to see one. There are reports of a particular mermaid who sits combing her long hair on a rocky island in the middle of the River Shannon. Those who see her will apparently die within one year. Despite their beauty, you should be wary of encountering these marine faeries!

In some parts of Ireland, mermaids are called merrows (*muiroigh*); a word derived from the Irish *muir* (sea) and *oigh* (maid). Merrows are a little different from other mermaids around the world. They can have many forms, varying from the well-known mermaid (human from the waist up with a fish tail) to rarer forms, such as being covered from head to toe in green scales. In most accounts, however, merrows are described as having a human form with flat feet and webbed fingers. You'd have to look very closely to spot them, but remember to watch out for flat-footed friends wearing gloves!

As with classic mermaids, female merrows are believed to be captivating and very beautiful. In contrast, male merrows are described as very ugly, with porcine (pig-like) features – a little easier to spot!

Lí Ban is the most famous Irish mermaid because she became a saint.

Stories about mermaid marriages are common in coastal counties. The O'Flahertys, O'Sullivans and MacNamaras are believed to be descendants of a marriage between a human and a mermaid.

In some tales, mermaids are children who survived an accident at sea, were rescued by mermaids and raised in Tír faoi Thoinn, the land beneath the waves.

There are carvings of mermaids in many Irish abbeys and churches, including Kilcooley Abbey and Clonfert Cathedral.

The Northern Lights

Everyone had gathered by the pier in great excitement – it was the best place to see the green and dark pink lights in the sky. It was a crisp evening, and people huddled close together as darkness fell around them. The northern lights were rare, but in the north-west, when the winter days were clear and bright, the shimmering waves of light could be seen for miles.

John looked up and clutched his sister's hand. There was silence around them as they all gazed at the colours that lit up the sky. It was magical, like something out of a dream.

Then John heard a gentle splash. He looked down at the sea; everyone else continued to stare up in awe. John crouched down and peered into the water...

The most beautiful woman he had ever seen was swimming in the water. Her skin glistened. Her long hair shone. The lights reflecting on the water made her large eyes glow.

The woman swam gracefully to the edge of the pier to look at the sky. John moved towards her. *Is she real?* he wondered.

John leaned over further to look closer. Suddenly, he lost his footing and felt the ground go from underneath him, and he fell into the water!

Down, down, down he went.

The ice-cold water filled up his boots; his overcoat was heavy, and the weight brought him down even faster. He spluttered and coughed before shutting his mouth

and holding what was left of his breath. John could hear his sister's voice crying out, calling his name.

He opened his eyes and looked up. Through the gloom, he could still see the dancing lights above the water. *I must keep moving; I must kick my feet*, he thought. He pushed his arms above his head.

Suddenly, a soft hand grasped his left arm and pulled. He felt a gentle tug and he was rising swiftly, up through the icy water.

It was the beautiful woman. Up close, he could see her flowing hair was golden. Her arms were long and pale, shimmering strangely in the light. And her legs... She had none! From the waist down, magnificent green scales glimmered on a graceful tail. They were the same colour as the lights.

She looked back at him and smiled. John was cold and his limbs were losing all feeling, but instantly he felt safe. In seconds she had brought him to the side of the pier, where they shot to the water's edge with a great splash.

A man called out and a rope was thrown into the water – just in front of them. The mermaid tied the rope around John's waist and tugged on it, firmly. He felt his body begin to rise out of the freezing water.

John looked back as they pulled him onto the pier and saw the mermaid looking up at him. She smiled, and her teeth shone like pearls in the coloured light. Then, in a moment she was gone – the tip of her tail was the last thing he saw before he fainted.

Every year on the same evening, John and his sister visit the same spot where he met the mermaid. As John looks out across the water, he knows that the mermaid is somewhere, watching them. He feels the same as he did when she brought him to the pier.

He feels safe.

LEPRECHAUN
·· LEIPREACHÁN ··

Small, solitary and speedy, the leprechaun is Ireland's best-known fae. If you have a keen eye, you might be lucky enough to catch a glimpse of one – but it's very unlikely you will be able to catch one! Catching one of these wily shoemakers is said to be nearly as difficult as finding the end of a rainbow. According to legend, if you catch a leprechaun and hold his gaze without blinking for a long time, he might reveal the location of his treasure or hand over his magic purse.

There's more to our national faerie than rainbows, crocks of gold, impressive beards and clay pipes (*dúidíní* or dudeens): they are believed by many to be descendants of the Tuatha Dé Danann, the deities of pre-Christian Ireland.

This miniature, solitary faerie is most often spotted in a hawthorn tree. If you listen closely, you might hear the tap, tap, tapping of a leprechaun making a tiny leather shoe. Leprechauns are known as skilled shoemakers who take pride in their work. They are only ever seen with one shoe, so if you come across the other shoe, you might be rewarded!

Most sources state that leprechauns are mischievous creatures, but they have also been known to reward kind people with good fortune, or a magic purse and a coin that reappears. (Note: the coin turns to dust if it is misused, so be sure to spend it on something good!)

Leprechauns are so popular that Ireland has its own Leprechaun Museum.

Leprechauns were first described in their famous green coats in Ancient Legends of Ireland, *a book by Lady Jane Wilde (Oscar Wilde's mother), published in 1888.*

Walt Disney completed research for his famous film Darby O'Gill and the Little People *by reading the Schools Manuscripts Collection at the National Folklore Collection, which contains more than 350 accounts of leprechaun sightings.*

The Queen's Shoes

The hawthorn tree wasn't in bloom when the ribbons appeared. It was a cold, drizzly March morning as Seán set out to check his flock of sheep.

From across the field, he heard the sound of tapping. It sounded like someone mending a fence, but as he got closer, he realized it was coming from the old hawthorn tree. Tiny bows were tied delicately on the branches next to the trunk. They were a dazzling array of colours.

When Seán approached the tree, he saw a tiny shoe – beautifully crafted, but not yet finished. It was waiting for a tiny set of laces, made from one of the ribbons. He bent down to take a better look and was so amazed that he didn't mind the damp grass on his knees, nor the cold, wet drizzle of rain. He was reaching for a ribbon when he heard a voice.

"What do you think you're doing?"

Seán's knees gave way and he tumbled onto his side. He pushed himself up – and there before him was a tiny, wizened old man. He was finely dressed in dark tweed with a polished pair of tan boots. He had a clay pipe in one hand and a tiny hammer in the other.

"If everyone helped themselves to a ribbon, there'd be none for the Queen's shoes. Then I wouldn't get paid, my wife would be cross and the children would be upset."

"I'm – I'm sorry," Seán spluttered, still not believing what he saw in front of him.

"And don't even think about picking up the Queen's shoe. She'd smell human all over it if you did, and she'd never wear it."

"I was only admiring it. It's beautifully made," Seán said.

"Well, now we agree on one thing," the tiny man replied, picking up the shoe and putting it under his jacket. "I don't want the rain to ruin it."

"Yes, the weather is said to get worse."

"Well, what are you waiting for?" the old man said and shook his head. "Help me gather these ribbons before they get wet."

Seán untied the ribbons and handed them to the tiny man, hurriedly.

"I'm not sure which colour she'd prefer, so I need to show her all of them," the old man said thoughtfully. He held Seán's gaze for the briefest of moments, then he smiled. "You're one of the good ones. Most would ask for my gold or try to trick me, or worse!"

The next morning, Seán found a small basket of eggs with a green ribbon tied to the handle. To this day, he says the eggs are the best he's ever tasted. He swears that from that day forth his luck in life changed for the better.

GIANT
·· FATHACH, GRUAGACH, GRÚGACH ··

Irish giants are widely celebrated in Celtic folklore, especially in Northern Ireland. Most tales tell of their extraordinary height, their incredible strength and the dramatic fights they have between their kin.

Some of these legends were told as a way to explain standing stones, dolmens (megalithic tombs) and boulders – believed to have been built by powerful giants. The story of Fionn mac Cumhaill and the Scottish Giant is one of the most famous, and tells of the mythical creation of the Giant's Causeway, Lough Neagh and the Isle of Man.

> *The Book of Invasions contains many accounts of giants, including* Fir Bolg *(the first inhabitants of mythical Ireland) and* Fomorian *(monstrous beings who were described as giants and sea raiders).*
>
> *Irish giants like Charles Byrne (1761-1783) became famous in Britain when they toured in shows as living exhibitions. Byrne moved from County Derry to London and became known as the "Irish Giant" at 2.30 metres. When he died, his skeleton was put on display in the Hunterian Museum for over 200 years.*

The story goes that Fionn built the Giant's Causeway to walk across the narrow sea to challenge Bendonner, a Scottish giant, to a fight. Fionn picked up a massive piece of ground and hurled it at Bendonner, who was much bigger than him. It went over his head and fell into the Irish Sea, forming the Isle of Man. The huge hole left behind filled with water and formed Lough Neagh. Bendonner retreated to Fingal's Cave in Scotland, tearing up the causeway so Fionn couldn't follow him. He never set a gigantic foot in Ireland ever again.

Whether these tall tales are true is up to you to decide, but there's no denying that Irish giants did exist. In 2016, a study revealed that the highest proportion of real-life giants in the whole world came from Northern Ireland. Their extraordinary height was due to a rare genetic condition that caused gigantism. This condition was passed down to members of eighteen families – all of whom shared a common ancestor – including the famous Irish giant Patrick Murphy (1834–1862), who was believed to have been over 2.46 metres tall.

Stomping Ground

The town had been a quiet place to live for as long as anyone could remember. Nestled in the hills beside Lough Neagh, some might even call it sleepy, especially during the hazy summer months.

Early one morning, everyone woke with a start when an almighty noise shook the rooftops of the town. When the people ran outside, the noise grew louder. The ground began to shake beneath their feet.

STOMP, STOMP, STOMP.

With each STOMP, the hillside shook, trees fell and cattle scattered down the fields. The water in the lake began rolling in large waves.

Suddenly, the sun was blocked out by two colossal figures. They were arguing and cursing each other in loud, booming voices. Everyone rushed inside and hid under their beds – everyone except for a brave young boy and his grandmother. They stood behind a tree and watched from a safe distance.

"Just as I thought," the old woman sighed. "They're *grúgaigh*."

"You mean giants, Granny?"

"Yes, child, but *grúgaigh* are especially hairy giants, descended from the Fomorians. They are terrible troublemakers."

"Will they eat us?" the boy asked, watching in horror as one *grúgaigh* picked up a cow and popped it in his mouth. The giant's gulp was so loud it made the fish in the lake leap up before they fell back with a loud plop. The giant burped. The bellowing sound was followed by a terrible stench.

"Hold your breath, child," the old woman instructed, with her hand over her mouth. "I've got an idea."

The giants sat down in the field and, one by one, they picked up the cows and ate them! When the last one was gone, the giants lay down and fell into a deep sleep. Their snores were so loud they were heard across the whole county.

The boy and his grandmother tiptoed up to a field next to where the giants lay, which was where the old woman kept her beehives.

"Now, ladies," she whispered to her bees, "I need your help." She removed a comb from the first hive and told her grandson to stay behind and mind the others.

The boy stood in wonder as he watched his grandmother creep up to the sleeping giants and place the comb between them. She tiptoed back to the hives, light as a feather on her feet. "The stench of their breath and the sound of their snores will annoy the bees," she said with a wink.

The boy and his grandmother watched as the bees began to buzz loudly. Just as the old woman had predicted, the swarm began to fly – and circle the sleeping giants. One stung the first giant on his chin, while another stung the second giant on his left ear. The giants leapt up, cursing and punching the air.

BANG! The giants had punched each other at exactly the same time and fallen to the ground with a deafening crash. Furious at all the commotion, the bees rained down more stings on them. Then the old woman opened the hives and let the bees join their sisters...

Bellowing and covering their heads with their huge hands, the giants raced up the hill and were soon out of sight – never to return.

BANSHEE
· · BEAN SÍ · ·

Have you ever heard a bloodcurdling wail in the dead of night? A sound so terrifying it makes your hair stand on end and your blood run cold. If you have, then you will know what you heard was a *bean sí* (banshee). If you've never heard about the source of this unearthly sound, then brace yourself: what you are about to read will send shivers down your spine!

The banshee is a supernatural messenger of death. Her wailing is heard across the world, alerting people to a relative's death. One of Ireland's best-known faeries, the banshee is, according to some people, a human prophetess; while, to others, she is the ghost of a professional keener (singing mourner). Her message lets people know about a loved one's death and serves as a reminder to support the grieving family.

This restless faerie is said to take on three different forms: a beautiful young woman; an old hag with messy hair clutching a comb; and a stately woman. Usually seen dressed in a long, grey hooded cloak, she can move swiftly as if gliding across the land. Believed to have the ability to transform into a hare, a stoat, a weasel and a cat, the banshee must never be approached, especially if she drops her comb. Sometimes she appears as a face at the window in the middle of the night, a spooky reminder to always close your curtains!

Bean sí *translates as "faerie woman", "unearthly woman" or "woman of the faerie".*

A bodach is another faerie very similar to the banshee, but male in appearance. Also known as bodach glas, fear liath *(grey man) or the grey spectre, he will sometimes appear three times, in order to make his point!*

Some believe that the banshee is a goddess of sovereignty, mourning the loss of land stolen from Irish chiefs and clans by intruders and invaders.

A Cry in the Dead of Night

It had been three weeks since the lady of the house had been struck down with a terrible fever. The doctor visited many times, but there was no more he could do for her. The family were summoned and warned that it may soon be time to say goodbye.

Her grandchildren came and sat with her, holding her small hand. They told her the wonderful stories she had shared with them many years before – local stories of incredible magical creatures. The King of the Cats who marched down the main street; the Kavanagh girl who transformed into a hare; the magical horses seen coming out of the lake and the flickering lights over the bog.

Over and over, the woman asked to see her youngest son. He was on his way – his carriage speeding through the night – but had a long road ahead.

At her bedside, her eldest son and her two daughters watched and waited. The lady lay still, her breathing laboured. In the sorrowful silence, a distant sound of beautiful music was heard. It was coming from outside – and it was getting louder. It was a haunting tune, unfamiliar yet gentle and comforting.

No one could understand where the music was coming from or who was playing it. But something about it brought them back to a time when their mother told them stories by the fire at night. It was as if their mother was sending them a message.

The children looked out of the window and saw their brother's carriage in the distance. The horses galloped across the bridge, around the sharp bend towards the winding road up to the estate. The music seemed to grow louder in time to the horses' steps. The sound and sight were captivating, and the whole family turned to watch.

All of a sudden a wail rang out – a sound so terrifying it made their blood run cold and the hairs on their necks stand up. On the road, the horses rose up, whinnying loudly. The carriage nearly toppled on its side. The lantern fell and smashed to smithereens, plunging the scene into darkness.

The beautiful music had stopped. A loud knock was heard at the window, followed by another and another. The wailing continued – an eerie, mournful and persistent cry. The horses reared up again and the carriage jolted forwards. When the family finally turned back to the old lady, her spirit had gone. She was at peace.

But the haunting music remained in the heads of the family for many days after her death. The eldest son said he had heard the very same tune years before when their great-aunt had died.

To this day, the family shares the old lady's fireside stories, enchanting her long line of relatives. But the most extraordinary is the tale of her death – and of the wail of the banshee.

THE GOOD PEOPLE

·· SÍDHE, AN LUCHT SÍ ··

According to many sources across folklore, Irish faeries object to being referred to as "faeries", so are commonly called the "good people" or the "good folk". You never know when they may be listening, so it's always recommended to refer to them by their chosen name – and to keep whatever you say complimentary!

Some believe the "good people" reside under faerie mounds or beneath hawthorn trees; others believe that they live freely among us, sometimes passing as humans. There are also reports of faeries protecting ancient sites such as ruins, as well as inhabiting woods, lakes, bogs and wells. Faeries can take different forms and are often able to shapeshift (mainly into hares, birds or cats) or become invisible. You never know when a faerie might be near!

The start of the seasons is thought to be a liminal time when faeries are more likely to enter our world – and are also more likely to snatch humans and take them back to their world. There are many tales of people being woken during the night to be taken to a faerie dance – returning in the early hours of the morning, tired from a night of merriment. Some people only return years later, or choose to stay in the faerie world forever. The start of summer (*Bealtaine*, the first of May) and winter (*Samhain*, the first of November) are major celebrations in Ireland, and they are popular times for faeries to appear freely amongst us.

At other times of the year, faeries are said to be visible only to people who possess "second sight" (the ability to see into the future). People who can communicate with the "good people" are called *síofraí*, which translates as "in the fairies". If you are not one of these people, it's considered bad luck to talk about the faeries too much or to seek them out. If they want to interact with humans, they will find you!

Belief in faerie abductions was so strong that people sometimes pretended to be a victim of one only to return years later. These were known as "faerie swindles" and were often used as a way to escape a threat to life or a false promise.

Faerie darts (iarógaí sídhe) are small arrows used as a form of revenge on miserly humans or their animals. If an animal becomes sick or a cow stops producing milk, people thought they might have been shot by one. Ancient flint arrowheads were often mistaken for faerie darts.

Don't Stop the Dance

The music was beautiful. It sounded old, as though it was from an ancient land, but familiar too, as if it had been played to her as a child, or in a dream.

Had it been a dream? She didn't think so.

The music stayed with her morning, noon and night. At first she tried to escape it, but soon it filled her every waking thought. She longed to be back there, amongst the "good people", circling, spinning, tripping lightly across the floor. When she was with them, she felt part of everything.

She hadn't believed the stories of people being taken by the faeries for a merry night of dance and returning with no memory of where they'd been. Now she knew that those people had wanted to keep it all for themselves. She felt the same. The "good people" were hers and they loved her, treated her like a queen. "Don't drink or eat anything," the stories urged. One morsel or sip would mean no return.

The rain never ceased that winter, and the days stretched out with tasks and stories she'd heard a thousand times. When it got too much, she'd close her eyes and remember the events of the night before: their captivating music, their dancing, their magnificent clothes and the way they spun her around, making her laugh. She'd close her eyes at the dinner table, during chores, on the way to the market and even when Tom came calling.

Soon, she couldn't keep her feet still – she'd tap in time to the rhythm of the music in her mind. She skipped when no one was looking. She closed her ears when her parents scolded and told her she was becoming drawn, thin and sickly. Couldn't they see she was full of life? She had seen how they lived – these wonderful folk others were scared of. The "good people" were kind and funny. Yes, they were full of magic, but it was special – not scary. And they had welcomed her.

She decided that when they came knocking that night, she would remain in the faerie realm. She'd hidden the shining silver shoes they had given her, but tonight she would put them back on. She'd dance and sing and laugh. When she sat down at their banquet, she would sip the wine and eat their fine food.

That night she waited for the light knock on the window. Three gentle taps and she was gone forever. Spellbound.

THE CHARMER

·· GANCANAGH, GEANCÁNACH ··

Beguiling and bewitching with a soothing voice, this silver-tongued faerie is said to be the most beautiful of all the "good people". But beware – this charmer is a master of smooth talking and seduction. Known as the "love talker", or *gancanagh*, this mysterious faerie will leave you lovesick and heartbroken after just one encounter.

This shapeshifter takes the form of a tall, gorgeous man, described as "easy on the eye". Well dressed with good posture, he holds a short clay pipe (*dúidín*), which he never smokes. He appears out of thin air, often right behind you, without a sound – and he does not cast a shadow. He seems friendly and familiar and he will whisper softly into your ear. His voice is gentle and seductive. No matter how hard you resist, he will cast a spell on you.

Folktales describe this charmer as an outcast of the faerie world, but the wrong he is accused of having committed varies from one story to another. In some tales, the *gancanagh* had his heart broken and never recovered, and so he chose to rove the mortal and faerie worlds alone. Human men who chase after women are also reported to have encountered this faerie.

The charmer is not just a smooth talker – he is also said to have a scent in his skin that is instantly addictive to humans. To prevent intoxication and ward off this beautiful, tricky faerie, you can wear a piece of iron around your neck or carry a twig of mistletoe or rowan at all times.

The gancanagh *is said to belong to the leprechaun family, even though he is tall and wiry.*

Stories of the charmer may have inspired Oscar Wilde to write his famous novel The Picture of Dorian Gray.

W. B. Yeats also wrote about this mysterious seducer in his folk tales, often alluding to his appearance to milkmaids and shepherdesses.

A Familiar Stranger

Nora Loftus was a quick-witted, good-tempered and beautiful young woman with flaming red hair. She turned many heads, but always said she was too young to worry about matters of the heart. Her parents agreed: there was time enough for her to marry, and when she did it would be a good match.

One fateful evening, Nora returned home shaking and crying after meeting a mysterious stranger on the road. She said she had felt his presence before she saw him – a handsome stranger who seemingly appeared out of thin air. He had made no sound as he approached her. Greeting her by name, he said he had been waiting a long, long time to meet her. Nora was immediately struck by his height, his posture and his fine clothes. His long fingers held a clay pipe – similar to her grandfather's – which he didn't light.

Nora had hesitated at first, a little dazed by his presence. But the air had smelled so sweet, like honeysuckle. His lively green eyes had held her gaze. No one had looked at her like that before. His smile made her dizzy – his teeth were so white, and his lips so full and red. Time stood still.

The stranger had reached out to Nora and whispered sweet nothings in her ear. He had taken her hand and kissed it, looking deep into her eyes. He declared his love for her there and then. There was no other woman for him but her. Nora had reached out to touch his face, and as she did so, she took a single blink. In that briefest of moments, her lover vanished. All that remained was a small clay pipe that Nora found lying by the side of the road.

As Nora recounted the tale to her parents, she shouted that her life would never be the same again. He had declared his love for her, and Nora knew they were fated. She had to find him. She searched high and low in every town and parish, clutching the small clay pipe.

Nora's encounter with the handsome stranger stole her of her senses. Some believe it was a young man from a faraway place; others state that he must have been someone from the landed gentry who was visiting the big house. But most believe he was the *gancanagh* – the dark faerie love-talker. What Nora doesn't know is that sightings of the handsome stranger were reported by many other women who passed along that road.

To this day, Nora Loftus walks the same road, searching for her faerie lover.

WILD WATER HORSES

· · EACH UISCE, CAPAILL UISCE · ·

The first thing you need to know about the *eacha uisce* is that wild horses couldn't tempt me to ride one. Not to be confused with seahorses, these supernatural water spirits are shapeshifters that can take the form of a horse, a pony or, more rarely, a man. They are often found by lakes, loughs and coasts and are *very* dangerous.

When *eacha uisce* appear as horses, they are often spotted with a gleaming saddle and bridle – ready to lure a rider onto their backs. They are bewitching, with their pristine coats, flowing creamy-white manes and bright, alert eyes. But if someone is foolish enough to mount one, the horse will gallop into the sea, dragging the rider beneath the waves. Once in the water, these tricky equine faeries will disappear with a large flash and a loud bang.

The Scottish equivalent of the *eacha uisce* is the kelpie. They are just as dangerous, and

even more malevolent, but prefer to haunt rivers, waterfalls and fjords. They take the form of a horse, but sometimes a woman too, and are often heard howling and wailing just before a storm – a little like the Irish banshee.

Eacha uisce feature in many stories of haunted lakes and loughs as cautionary tales to keep children away from water but also to treat horses well – as you never know when they might be faerie horses!

The River Shannon and Lough Swilly are said to be haunted by eacha uisce, *and Loch Lomond in Scotland is believed to be home to a kelpie called Lizzie.*

From a distance, breaking waves often look like white horses' manes, and crashing waves can sound like galloping horses' hooves. Could this be the source of the eacha uisce *stories?*

As Swift as the March Wind

Pat Lehane was a deeply suspicious man who was convinced that everyone was out to trick him. He'd fallen out with all his family and friends over money and land. He was so sure his neighbours were grazing cattle in his fields that he took to patrolling his land in the dead of night, so as to not have to share a single blade of grass.

One cool night, when the moon was full, Pat went out to check his land and walked as far as the edge of Cullane Lake, grumbling to himself. He stopped mid-stride when he saw the most incredible sight before him: a beautiful mare and her foal walking out of the lake and into his field without making a sound. He watched in wonder as they grazed silently. They were majestic horses, fine of limb with glossy coats and bright eyes.

"So these are the thieves!" he said. The mare looked up and moved away swiftly. Quick as a flash, Pat rushed towards them. The mare bolted – but he caught the foal in his strong, mean grip. The foal cried out and the mare responded from the lake with a loud whinnying. It was a mournful sound that made Pat shake, but nothing would make him release the magical creature.

The foal was fast and strong, and grew to be a fine racehorse who won every race Pat entered him into. People came from far and wide, and paid good money to see the faerie horse. Pat boasted that his horse was as swift as the March wind and as strong as a giant. He needed a double harness to secure him.

Pat's old neighbour Peg warned him that no good would come of keeping the faerie horse. "As soon as he gets a chance, that horse will return to the water – and take you with him! No double harness will stop him," she said. But Pat paid no heed, especially when he was making so much money from the faerie horse.

One evening, Pat was returning from the *Lughnasa* races, tired out from all the excitement. His horse had been the talk of the races, and he was feeling very proud.

Pat relaxed the reins for a moment – and in that moment, the horse saw his chance, and bolted. The horse did indeed gallop faster than the March wind, and was indeed as strong as a giant, and he pulled Pat down the steep road straight to Cullane Lake. Pat tried to jump off, but his legs were stuck – as if by magic.

Pat heard a loud whinnying coming from the lake, and his horse responded, moving faster towards the water. The sound of galloping hooves and whinnying grew louder and louder. Then, without the slightest hesitation and without the slightest sound, the horse leapt into the lake. A flash of lightning shot across the valley.

Neither Pat nor the faerie horse was ever seen again, though his neighbours say they sometimes hear whinnying in the middle of the night.

CHANGELING

·· IARLAIS OR *SÍOFRA* ··

Human children have always fascinated the "good people", especially babies. Cautionary tales of bright, bonny babies being snatched and swapped for faerie babies – or, worse, old, bad-tempered faeries – have been passed down through the generations.

Not all abductions result in a "changeling" replacing the stolen child, however. Sometimes, a piece of wood known as a "stock" will be left in the snatched baby's cradle. The stock will resemble the child for a short period – giving the faerie enough time to get away. Adults can also be swapped for changelings, who will resemble the stolen human but will be quiet and sullen. (Note: they might just be the real person in a bad mood!)

If you suspect a changeling is in your midst, the best way to get rid of them is to surprise them into revealing their age. For example, by doing something unusual like boiling eggshells. A changeling can't resist telling you that "in all their one hundred and fifty years they have *never* seen such a sight", or something like that. Once they've revealed their age, they will either fly up the chimney or sprint out of the door.

Daisy chains are an effective way of protecting against faerie abduction, as are foxgloves, a four-leaf clover, St John's wort, rowan berries and ash branches. If plants play havoc with your hay fever, you can place iron, salt or bread and water around your house, or leave an item of a parent's clothing on a child's bed. The sound of bells can also be used to keep changelings at bay.

If all else fails and the changeling won't leave, you can enjoy the fact that they are gifted musicians and present them with a fiddle or pipes!

> *In the past, changelings were often used to explain health issues in babies. So remember the next time a baby is kicking up an almighty fuss, they could be a changeling – or they could just be teething!*
>
> *Stories about changelings were often told as a warning to ensure children were careful when walking home after dark.*
>
> *The name for foxgloves comes from "folk's glove", because this flower was believed to have been worn by the faeries.*

The Faerie Switch

When Donal and Brendan were born, they were the talk of the village. One baby would have been a blessing, but two healthy boys was an unexpected delight.

The twins shared a wooden cot, sleeping top to tail. People came from far and wide to admire them. "How can you tell them apart?" they'd ask. But when they looked closer, they could see some small differences: the shape of their eyes, the curve of their cheeks and the volume of their wails.

All that changed on *Bealtaine* when the babies' parents were outside feeding the hens. Afterwards, they swore a dark shadow had fallen across the yard in the middle of the day, and the babies suddenly began to cry. In the distance, they saw a figure slip away from the house and across the field.

When they ran inside, the babies wouldn't cease their crying. The parents tried many things, but nothing would calm them. The babies seemed to be changed in some way.

Three weeks later, a travelling tailor was hired by the babies' father to mend his jacket and trousers. The parents went out to cut turf and asked the tailor to watch the boys as they were fussing. The minute they were gone, the babies stopped their wailing. The tailor was quietly sitting by the fire sewing when all of a sudden baby Donal turned to his brother and spoke.

"Do you remember the old songs?"

"I do, and many others besides," replied little Brendan.

"Get out your fiddle there and I'll dance a jig," Donal said, leaping out of the cot.

The tailor looked on in wonder as the other baby jumped out of the cot and picked up the fiddle in the corner – and began to play.

The tailor gasped when he saw that the babies' faces looked older and sharper.

Brendan's music was magnificent and Donal sprang up and danced a jig. The tailor had never seen such an accomplished dancer. But just before the parents returned, Brendan stopped playing. "Whist. They're coming back."

The changelings jumped back into the cot so fast they nearly toppled it over. The crafty faeries made him swear blind he wouldn't tell a soul. When the parents entered, the babies began crying again, their faces morphing back to regular babies.

The tailor knew he must act fast. He instructed the parents

to sit down and not to move. He raced over to the fire and heated a small shovel – and then, quick as anything, he put it under the cot. The parents shrieked, but no sooner was the red-hot shovel under the cot than the two babies leapt out of it, cursing. They ran out of the door as fast as a March hare – but not before the parents saw their faces change to the sharp features of faeries. They couldn't believe their eyes.

Moments later, a strange woman appeared at the door and flung their own two babies back into the room. The parents caught them and gazed in amazement at their beautiful children, returned safely home.

FAERIE CAT
· · CAT SÍDHE · ·

Cats have long been revered and feared in equal measure. Throughout history, they have been lauded as gods by the ancient Egyptians, suspected of being the feline companions of supernatural beings such as witches, and said to be almost immortal – to have nine lives, rather than one. They have long been associated with psychic powers and the ability to see ghosts, most likely because they are nocturnal and can see very well in the dark with their gleaming, reflective eyes.

In Ireland, the myth of a cat's nine lives may come from stories of the *cat sídhe*. These faerie cats are said to be larger than the average cat, often black with a white bib, and are able to change between cat and human form. This ability to transform gives them freedom to sneak into places undetected, as well as the opportunity to listen in on secret conversations or to make a quick escape. Many cultures report stories about witches turning into black cats, but these shapeshifting faeries are only able to transform from a human form to a cat and back eight times. On their ninth transformation, it is believed that the *cat sídhe* become trapped in their feline forms.

Traditionally, the *cat sídhe* were also feared because of the belief that they could steal the soul of a deceased person. If a large cat appeared at a wake, it was often chased away by the mourners. They would also keep guard beside the coffin before the burial to make sure their loved one was protected from the faerie cat.

Some people still believe it is bad luck to talk near a cat in case it is a witch trying to learn your secrets.

In some countries, it's considered unlucky if a black cat crosses your path. In Ireland, it's often a sign of good luck!

The Cave of the Cats in County Roscommon is said to be an entrance point to the faerie world, and traditionally is where **Samhain (Halloween)** *was first celebrated.*

The King of the Cats

Brian the Bard had completely forgotten it was *Samhain*, but everyone in the town had remembered the saucer of milk for the *cat sídhe*. Brian was as sensible a man as you'd meet in a week's walking. But when his own cat tried to remind him by miaowing loudly by the door and rattling the saucer, he got annoyed and shooed the old tom away.

So no one was surprised when they heard what happened to the old bard that night.

He was snoozing by the fire when there was a loud knock on the door.

"Who's there?" he asked, but there was no answer. This went on three times.

When he opened the door, there was no one there at first. But then a very large black cat slunk up to the entrance and reared up on its hind legs, revealing a white bib of fur. Brian was very surprised and a little unsure of what to do, but just as he went to close the door, the cat spoke.

"You have less than a minute to put out a saucer of milk."

"I must be dreaming," the old man muttered. "This can't be real."

"I'm as real as the whiskers on my face. You have less than a minute to put out the milk."

Brian laughed and shook his head.

"This is no joking matter! The King of the Cats has passed on. The funeral procession is coming, and you must leave out milk or it will be seen as the greatest disrespect."

Then Brian's own cat rose up from his place by the fire. "If the King of the Cats is dead," he said, "they will need a new king. I must go to help them find one."

Brian staggered back. "W-what?"

"Old man, you have been warned," his old cat urged. "If you don't put out the milk on *Samhain*, the King's cats will have their revenge." With that, he raced towards the fireplace and disappeared up the chimney.

The smell of singed fur filled Brian's nostrils, and it made him spring into action. Grabbing a saucer, he poured the last drops of milk from his jug, before a procession of nine black cats came into the road. Each black cat had a white bib, and they marched on their hind legs towards him, carrying a small coffin. Brian sighed with relief as the procession walked by.

No one else saw the large black cats that night.

The next morning, Brian woke to the sound of miaowing at his door. He went outside to find his cat drinking milk from the saucer. The old cat strolled into the house without a second glance – there was a small golden crown on his head.

FAERIE DOG

· · CÚ SÍDHE · ·

You may think that a faerie dog sounds adorable – but think again! These massive hounds should never be approached, especially after dark. Most faerie dogs, or *cúnna sídhe*, are said to be as large as a donkey or even a bull, with black shaggy fur, gigantic paws and fiery eyes. Their barks are so thunderously loud that there are stories of sailors aboard ships in the Atlantic hearing their beastly howls!

Irish faerie dogs are fiercely loyal and protective of other faerie folk, and are said to be the guard dogs of the *sídhe*. These magical hounds come out at night to guard sacred places such as faerie mounds, keeping them safe from trespassing humans.

They are also thought to act as protectors of the dead, as many sightings of these huge hounds are reported during *Samhain*, or Halloween. The faerie dogs are believed to guard souls as they wander freely for the night. They're not *always* a scary sight, though, as they have also been known to guide lost travellers to safety when they have been instructed by the faeries. Still, a word to the wise: don't go traipsing around sacred sites after dark!

Cúnna sídhe are also known to appear and disappear at will, usually during a storm. They often appear silently, just after a flash of lightning. It's considered unlucky to see a faerie dog, so whatever you do, don't follow one! It could be trying to lead you to the underworld or draw you under a spell.

Faerie dogs appear in many great Irish legends, including those of hero Fionn mac Cumhaill, leader of the legendary band of warriors, the Fianna. Fionn famously had two faerie dogs, Bran and Sceolán, who used their magical powers and great strength to protect him. Some believe that the *cúnna sídhe* are descended from the god Crom Dubh's legendary hunting dogs, who were known as the Hounds of Rage.

Cúnna sídhe are different to *púcaí*, who sometimes take the form of a black dog. Faerie dogs do not speak, unlike *púcaí*, who are known for being chatterboxes.

In parts of Britain, especially Cornwall, spectral hounds were known as yell-hounds, yeth-hounds or wish hounds. These terrifying ghostly dogs are believed to have been inspired by tales of the hounds of Odin, brought to Britain by the Vikings.

Hush Now

Have you ever heard phantom crying – the mournful sound of a baby wailing – but when you search for the upset infant, there's none to be found?

It was twilight on an autumn evening when Willie John Bradley heard a baby wailing. His own brood were adults now, but the old man was known for having the gift of soothing a crying baby and rocking it gently to sleep. Some might have described him as some kind of "sleep doctor". Teething, colic, wind, pure crankiness – nothing fazed him.

He searched his house and garden, in case someone had left a crying infant for him to mind. He followed the crying and found it was coming from the field behind his house. He rarely entered the field because of the faerie mound – but he always paid his respects to the "good people" when he passed.

As a child he'd been dared to race around the mound three times. When he got to the second round, he lost the nerve. Some said he'd missed his chance to see a leprechaun or a faerie queen. Over the years, folk had reported hearing voices inside the mound; some even heard music. But Willie John knew it was best not to disturb them. It was rumoured that faerie dogs roamed the field, guarding the mound. He believed it. Many a time he'd heard their thunderous barks late at night.

When Willie John reached the field, the crying increased. He approached the mound – his heart racing and sweat pouring off him. Instinctively, he started to sing the lullaby he sang to his children. Within a minute, the crying had lessened.

Willie John jumped in fright when a massive hound appeared from inside the mound. He was gigantic, the size of a bullock. The hound walked over and sniffed him: first his boots, then his knees and finally his trembling hands. The hound looked into his eyes and held his gaze. Willie John knew then that this was a faerie hound. His mouth went dry. The dog gave three loud barks.

A young woman walked out of the faerie mound carrying a sniffling baby. Willie John recognized her as Honora Mulcahy. Honora and her son had been missing for a week, and folk had speculated that she had been taken to the other side to mind a faerie baby. What they didn't know was that Honora had fallen in the field and the hound had brought her to the "good people" to recover.

Willie John felt the blood drain from his face. He was shivering when Honora bent down and handed him her baby – who sighed and fell asleep instantly. She turned to the faerie dog and patted him on the head.

"Thank you. You can go home now. Let *them* know I've returned safely. I'm in good hands."

SELKIE

·· MAIGHDEAN MHARA ··

The selkie may look like a common seal, but these marine faeries are believed to be the souls of drowned people come back to live among us. Using sealskins to live underwater, these dearly departed souls shed their sealskins when on land and become human. They are able to survive out of the water for short periods of time.

Selkie sealskins are made into cloaks, capes or *cochaillíní draíochta* (magical capes), which selkies can put on and take off, and which allow them to swim underwater and travel through strong currents. In many folktales, selkies' garments are discovered and hidden by humans, which prevents the faeries returning to sea.

Selkies come to land every ninth day of the month to dance on the shore – so keep an eye out for them – but you must maintain a safe distance at all times. They are far more beautiful than humans, so most mortals who encounter them are mesmerized. Many selkie stories focus on a marriage between a smitten human and a selkie. The children of these unions have small webs between their fingers and between their toes. It is said that women can summon up a male selkie to be their new love by shedding seven tears into the sea, but they must be unhappily married to a mortal man at the time.

Most selkie sightings have been documented in Scotland, though stories of selkies are very common in Ireland too. In some parts of the country, the mere sight of a selkie is considered very unlucky. Darker tales describe them appearing at midsummer to lure unsuspecting mortals to their deaths with their large, captivating eyes.

Selkies are often seen before a storm, shipwreck or drowning. If a selkie's blood is shed, a terrible storm will occur and the selkie folk will lure sailors or fishermen to their deaths. So steer clear of these marine faeries and never steal their sealskin coats, capes or fancy hats!

As these shapeshifting faeries look like seals in water and humans on land, selkies are sometimes called seal maidens.

The ancient Irish Conneely family is said to be descended from selkies. In Connemara, seals are sometimes known as "Conneelys".

In the Scottish Highlands and islands, selkies are called roane *(which comes from "seal" in Scottish Gaelic). The Irish name Rónán means "little seal".*

Washed Ashore

Life on the islands off the coast of Ireland can be lonely, especially in the depths of winter. Many a man or woman has gazed out to sea wondering what it would be like to have someone to keep company with. On these islands, if you don't work the land, you work the sea, and both are lonely, difficult jobs – particularly when the winds are howling and the waves are crashing around you.

After a terrible storm, an island man was on the beach when he saw a woman lying motionless on the shore. Her face was covered by seaweed and, in her hand, she clutched a dark cloak. When he peered closer, he saw it was a sealskin. It smelled of salt.

The woman's chest rose and fell. The man called to her softly, but she didn't stir or speak. All he could hear was the rhythmic sound of the waves.

Stories of selkies were common, but the man had never quite believed them until this moment. He knew this beautiful woman would need to return home to the sea ... eventually. For now, he would take her home and help her to recover.

The man gathered the woman up carefully and carried her back to his house. For three days and nights, she didn't move. When she finally woke, she instantly looked for her sealskin. At first, the man intended to return it to her, but he didn't want her to leave. So he hid it in the rafters. The woman knew he was a good man, but she could smell his shame.

Life on the shore was easier than at sea. The pair got on and soon fell in love. Seven years went by and the man was happy. His wife was kind and gentle, and they had four beautiful children – three boys and a girl. But each month on the evening of the ninth, when selkies were said to come ashore to dance, the woman would end the evening by singing a mournful song.

One morning, while the man was out, their daughter asked why her father always looked up at the rafters when her mother sang, as if he was expecting something to fall down. Quick as a flash, the woman clambered up to the rafters and pulled down what looked like a dark blanket. A large grey cloak landed with a thud on the table. It smelled of the sea, even after all these years.

The woman inhaled and let out a deep sigh. She kissed her child and told her to look after the family. Then she wrapped the cloak around her and sprinted out of the door.

The man was in his boat when he spotted his wife running to the shore as if her life depended on it. His daughter was sprinting after her.

The woman ran into the sea. When she was waist-deep, she dived under the water. The daughter raced into the waves, shouting. A large, sudden wave dragged the girl under and tossed her back onto the shore.

The man picked her up and said gently, "Darling, you are safe."

He shouted out to the sea, thanking his wife for returning their daughter to safety. The selkie woman was never seen again.

POOKA
· · PÚCA · ·

The pooka is one of Ireland's best-known faeries. This shapeshifting sprite can transform into various creatures, from an eagle to a hare, but usually takes the form of a horse or a goat. Some describe the creature as part goat, part bull, or a strange man with a donkey's ears or a goat's tail – although this is a rarer version of the story. In some parts of Ireland, all faeries or strange creatures are referred to as *púcaí*.

Full of merriment, with a touch of malice, the pooka appears on lonely nights in remote places to play tricks. This rogue rascal is known for appearing out of the dark, lifting a person onto his back and sprinting across the countryside before returning them to exactly the same spot. The rider is flung back onto the road, usually without any memory of their adventure. Other tales tell of the pooka climbing on a person's back and making them leap over the hedges.

The pooka has the gift of the gab and is known for causing mischief and mayhem. *Púcaí* can also play a protective role, especially to kind and generous folk – and may use their talk to help, protect and even give prophecies about the future.

Some believe that the pooka appears through the cracks of rivers, springs and waterfalls. There are many place names around the country named after this legendary trickster's appearance: Poll an Phúca (pool of the *púca*), Castlepook (the goblin's castle), Carrigapooka Castle, County Cork, and Artane in County Dublin was originally named Pollaphúca.

So next time you are in a secluded spot, watch out for this mysterious and clever sprite. Though if you are taken on a gallop, remember they do not like metal or iron, which is why you'll never find stirrups on a pooka! It's not all bad though; the pooka often gives the rider the gift of sense (*ciall*) and cleverness at the end of the journey!

Some believe that stories of the pooka originate from prehistoric times and were inspired by the woolly mammoth.

Legend has it that the last High King of Ireland, Brian Boru, used a magic bridle to conquer and ride a pooka in place of a horse.

The name pooka, or púca, derives from poc, the Irish word for a male goat. The pooka's sacred day is 1 November – just after Halloween night.

At Full Pelt

It's been said that you'd hear him before you'd see him. You'd be walking home in the wee hours, minding your own business, most likely after returning from a party or a wake. He'd appear beside you and start talking – a voice both strange and yet familiar. You wouldn't see him at first, just hear his constant chatter. He'd drop something at your feet and as you bent down to retrieve it for him, he'd gather you on his back, quick as a flash, and take off like a hare. You'd have no choice but to hold on tight!

It would be then that you'd notice what a peculiar creature he was. You'd wonder if you'd banged your head or were dreaming. But the chill of the air would keep you alert to the fact that you were sitting on the back of a creature racing at full speed through the night.

As terrifying as this sounds, there would be something likeable about him, and you knew if you kept him talking and minded your manners, he'd cause you no harm. That feeling would make you grip on harder, and you might even enjoy the ride.

When you realized that he was heading for the cliffs, you'd yell, but he'd stop and turn before you got there. You would think it wasn't possible for him to go any faster, but he'd accelerate and you'd be off again, swerving too close for comfort as you heard the sound of the waves crashing against the rocks below.

You'd shut your eyes for a second and when you opened them, you'd shake your head in disbelief as you realized you were back where you started. He'd skid to a halt and send you flying. You'd land with a thump on the road and stare at him in amazement as he changed form into a large goat then disappeared in a flash of light, leaving behind only the sound of his lingering laughter.

When folks asked, you couldn't be sure if he was a goat, a dog or a horse. Or if you'd dreamed the whole thing.

TREE FAERIE

·· SÍDHE SCEICHE OR SÍDHE DARACH ··

As far back as ancient times, people have treated trees like royalty. In ancient Greece, tree spirits were called dryads, or wood nymphs, and were said to take the form of a beautiful woman. In England, tree faeries are often called oak men or green men. In other countries, folk believe the trees themselves are magical creatures that can talk and move their branches.

In Ireland, the Celts believed that the roots of trees connected our world to the otherworld. Every tree was thought to have a resident spirit or faerie, sometimes called an oakshee or skeaghshee. When the Celts cleared a wood for settlements, they would ensure that a lone tree was left in each area because they valued the role trees played in life and nature. These lone trees are particularly revered as they are believed to be markers for sacred places and portals to the faerie world.

If you spot a tree faerie, you'll notice their wizened appearance and slight stature. But it is very rare to spot them, as they dress in browns and greens for camouflage. Though often called oakshee, these faeries can be found in trees all over the country – and especially in hawthorns. If you fall asleep under a hawthorn on *Samhain*, *Bealtaine* or Midsummer's Night, you might encounter one!

Rowan trees are said to protect a house from bad luck and ill-treatment from faeries.

Pollen findings suggest hawthorn trees have been in Ireland since 6000 BCE. In modern times, planning regulations have been changed to protect lone hawthorn trees.

The word "door" is said to come from dair, *the Irish for oak, because these trees were believed to be portals, or doors, to other worlds.*

These guardian *sídhe* protect their homes fiercely. If you damage a tree – or, worse, cut it down – you and your family could be plagued by misfortune in the form of ill health and poverty.

If you want to stay on a tree faerie's good side, a gentle tap or knock on a tree is considered essential in order to gain their respect. Touching or knocking on wood is an old practice that shows respect to the guardian tree spirits, and sometimes can lead to good fortune.

The next time you have a run of bad luck, think back to the last time you hugged a tree, if ever. Or ask if any of your relatives ever damaged or chopped down a lone tree. This might well be the root of all your misfortune!

Hidden Treasure

Peggy looked around before entering the field to make sure no one had followed her. Coming to the faerie tree had started as a dare, but it soon became a habit. Peggy knew the others would laugh at her if they discovered that she came here every Friday, long after the dare was over.

They had sent her here to find treasure or gold coins, hidden under the tree by the skeaghshee. Peggy didn't find any, of course, because the treasure wasn't real. She had been brave, though, even though she'd felt shaky and sick. And now she kept coming back, but didn't know why…

It was very quiet – all Peggy could hear were the crows above loudly signalling their presence in the large trees that bordered the field. She remembered her grandmother's stories about the town, Skeaghanore, named after the large whitethorn tree that stood in the field – or hawthorn, as some folks said. Peggy preferred whitethorn, especially when the tree was in full bloom and the flowers could be seen from afar. She could smell the flowers the minute she set foot in the field.

She crossed the field with long strides, picking up her pace before sprinting to the middle, where she stopped and gazed up at the beautiful whitethorn tree. "Hello," she whispered, tapping lightly on the bark. "Ever since I came here, the others have stopped calling me names or daring me to do things." Peggy sat down and felt herself relax against the tree trunk. "Things are better now."

She stretched, yawned and, in minutes, was fast asleep. She had been asleep for less than ten minutes when a tiny, wizened man climbed down from the tree without a sound.

The man crouched down to look closely at her. Peggy woke with a start and gasped.

"Don't be afraid, child," he said holding up his tiny hand. "I mean you no harm."

"Am I dreaming?" Peggy asked, staring at the man dressed all in brown and green. He was no bigger than her thumb and was wearing the smallest hat she had ever seen.

"No, Peggy."

"How do you know my name?"

"I heard the other children call you when you first came here."

"You – you were here then?"

"I'm always here."

"I haven't come to search for treasure," Peggy promised, jumping up.

"Of course not. You've already found the treasure," the little man replied.

"Excuse me?" spluttered Peggy.

"Your respect for the tree has been noticed," he said, walking slowly around the tree. "Each time you come, it gains strength."

Peggy followed him. "What gains strength? I haven't found the treasure. I … I just feel at home here – I feel safe."

"Faerie treasure is not always gold," the little man explained. When Peggy still looked confused, he raised his arms up to the tree. "As the tree grows in strength, so do you. The treasure you have found is wisdom and connection. It's made you brave; people have noticed. It's not magic that's warded off your bullies – it's the power of knowing yourself. That is the real treasure."

In a swirl of mist, the little man was gone.

HEADLESS HORSEMAN

· · DÚLACHÁN · ·

I can tell you this for nothing: there's nothing dull about the *dúllahán*! If you spot him in the distance fast approaching, don't lose your head – turn on your heel and run for the hills. The arrival of the *dúllahán* spells death, and it's best to steer clear of this faerie.

On his black steed, this headless horseman charges at full speed – his enormous stallion's galloping hooves quickening every pulse within earshot. His long black cloak billows in the wind behind him, while flames fire out of his stallion's nostrils. A terrifying sight!

The headless horseman doesn't speak, other than to shout the name of a person whose death is imminent. It's said that his voice is so deep and otherworldly that it seems to make time stand still. But rest assured: the *dúllahán* is only interested in cruel people who have committed despicable crimes.

In some tales, the horseman is depicted as a warrior who lost his head in battle and returns to roam the land in revenge. But most stories describe him as one of Crom Dubh's descendants, returning with a physical form to take souls for the ancient Celtic god. The Celts believed that heads were symbols of fertility and long life – especially when thrown into a well. Water from these wells was believed to possess life-giving properties. Celts also used their enemies' skulls to defend their sacred spaces. Quite a sight!

Unlike with other faeries, iron does not protect you from the *dúllahán*. You must carry gold to ward him off, so try to keep some gold coins or jewellery on you at all times.

The headless horseman features in many myths and legends all over the world, from German folktales to Celtic mythology.

Stories of the dúllahán were brought to America by Irish immigrants and are said to have inspired "The Legend of Sleepy Hollow".

You can still see stone-carved heads in a number of churches across Britain and Ireland, including Clonfert Abbey in County Galway.

At the Crossroads

No one was quite sure what age Bríd O'Malley was, but it was always a subject of much debate. It was said she had outlived three husbands, ten children and twenty-seven grandchildren. The island people were convinced she was a witch, but the people from her own village knew better.

On the eve of *Samhain*, when Bríd was just a slip of a thing, she was sent to deliver a parcel to a neighbour a few fields away. As she was returning home, she took a wrong turn on the crossroads. It was dark, and the moon cast an eerie light across the valley. The night was still and silent, deathly silent.

All of a sudden, Bríd heard the sound of distant hooves coming closer and closer. The sound grew louder, thundering, determined, almost deafening.

Bríd looked up and down the road, and there, racing down towards the crossroads, she saw a large man on the most enormous horse. The rider had a long, black cloak with a hood that hid his face. Bríd stumbled back against the brambles on the roadside. The tiny thorns scratched the backs of her legs, bringing her to her senses. With a quick leap, she was over the hedge and into the next field.

The horse was galloping at full speed and Bríd was sure he would have knocked her off her feet if she had stayed on the road. He came to a skidding halt, right beside her.

Peering through the hedgerow, Bríd could see the horseman was clutching something in his left hand. Bríd could not believe her eyes when she saw it was a man's head held aloft by thick, wavy hair. She bit her tongue to stop herself from crying out. She knew she was staring straight at the *dúllahán* – right after he had taken someone.

Every *Samhain*, fireside stories would feature the horrifying headless horseman. Bríd had never believed the old tales, but here the horseman was – right in front of her.

The head shook in the horseman's hand, the man's eyes staring at the exact spot where Bríd was hiding. Bríd couldn't help it – she let out a yelp and started to shake uncontrollably. The horseman turned to face her. He reached down and brought a finger in front of his hood to the space where his lips should have been. Bríd nodded in agreement – she would keep the *dúllahán's* secret.

When the local landowner went missing that night, the village was filled with tall tales; every-thing from escaping debts to a secret family in another county.

To this day, Bríd has kept the *dúllahán's* secret. And in return, the headless horseman has given her a gift – and allowed her to escape death completely.

SHAPESHIFTER
·· PISEOGAÍ ··

Stories of shapeshifting are found across the globe, from Armenia to the Philippines, and they also appear in Celtic, Greek and Norse mythology. Shapeshifters are similarly plentiful in Irish folklore, and stories often feature humans or faeries changing shape in order to make a thrilling escape. In many parts of the country, shapeshifters were called *piseogaithe*, or charm setters.

Though some stories tell of ordinary people changing into another form, most shapeshifters are members of the fae. Some faeries are born with the ability; others gain it through years of training, like wizards' apprentices. Shapeshifting is often used as a method of escape, but can also be inflicted on human beings as a form of punishment – such as when an evil person is transformed into a midge or a fly. These darker tales of wicked enchantments are well known, in particular "The Children of Lir". In this story, King Lir's four children were turned into swans by their jealous stepmother, Aoife.

Some shapeshifting faeries can only take two forms, such as the wild water horses who have a human and horse form. But most Irish shapeshifters take the form of a bird, hedgehog or hare. Others like the powerful Irish goddess the Morrigan have the ability to transform into a number of creatures: a crow, an eel, a heifer and a wolf. Some shapeshifters require an item of clothing or an object to change from, such as the selkies and their sealskins, while others can transform without any aid.

Shapeshifting is a dangerous activity for humans and faeries, because if the wind changes while you are in a different form, you are stuck in that form forever!

> *Some tales state that only women, especially old wise women, are able to shapeshift.*
>
> *If butter or cream disappeared from a farm, it was usually blamed on a shapeshifter or the local* bean feasa *- a woman of knowledge.*
>
> *Some faeries can only cast an illusion, known as a "glamour", to make it look like a transformation has occurred.*

Hare Raising

A large hare was spotted in the Kavanaghs' meadow, just by the woods. It was an extraordinary creature with incredible ears; bright, intelligent eyes and a gleaming russet coat. Anyone who was lucky enough to see it said it was strangely beautiful. What was really unusual was that the hare didn't sprint off the minute it saw you but would stand still and stare, as if it was about to speak.

When butter and eggs went missing around the town, people began to speculate. Tensions started to run high and tempers became frayed. When the hare was seen running at full pelt away from the hen house or the creamery and into the Kavanaghs' yard, most were sure they'd found the thief.

Biddy Ryan – the last *bean feasa* (woman of knowledge) – had been laid to rest just three

months before. Folk knew her wisdom must have been passed on, but no one knew where to – until now. Even her own people believed she had been a *piseogaí* and a shapeshifter. Everyone had kept their distance from the faerie woman – unless they needed a cure or a baby delivered safely. No one had ever seen Biddy leave after she visited a house, but many was the time an old hare was seen close by.

Mairín Kavanagh had just turned sixteen. She was a striking young woman with soft, russet hair – just like her late mother's. Biddy had delivered her as a baby, and they had often been seen speaking. With everyone else, she was quiet and kept to herself.

A local man, William O'Donnell, had taken a shine to Mairín and wished to marry her. But whenever he called to the house, Mairín was nowhere to be found. The third time, William left in a rage, certain that she was avoiding him. Each time he saw the hare race off across the fields as if it was running for its life.

Furious, William thought: if Mairín wouldn't marry him, he would make sure she wouldn't marry another. A week later, he bragged to all who would listen how his butter was the best it had ever been – it tasted different, much sweeter and creamier.

At the next full moon, he waited. He'd left the door ajar and crouched behind it. He saw the hare hop into his kitchen. When the hare leapt onto the table, there was an almighty clatter as an iron trap clasped down on its hind leg. The trap snapped open, knocking the hare in the face. The hare screamed – a sound so terrifying it sounded like a *bean sí*. William saw a cut on the hare's left cheek. It stopped and stared at him before fleeing.

Neither Mairín nor the hare was seen for a long time – nearly a year – until William's new wife went into labour. Mairín arrived at the door minutes before the baby was born, as the town's midwife. She had a bandage on her face. She did not speak to William, but he felt her quiet rage.

Every morning since Mairín's return, William has woken to a fresh cut across his cheek. William can't prove it, but he believes it is the shapeshifter seeking her revenge. Meanwhile, a russet hare is often seen in the fields around the town – running wild and free.

SHEERIE
·· TEIN SIONNIE OR TEIN SÍDHE ··

The sheerie is one of Ireland's lesser-known faes. Sinister and spiteful, it appears as warm, twinkling lights in bogs and other remote places to lead unsuspecting travellers astray. Whatever you do, don't be fooled by these dazzling lights, because the sheerie is one of Ireland's most malicious faeries.

Visible at dusk or after dark, these lights often appeal to weary travellers in search of a place to rest or a path to follow – who instead find themselves led into a watery grave in the soft, wet earth of the bog. The flickering lights entice the unsuspecting follower on a merry dance across treacherous terrain.

The lights can burst into flame or appear as luminous flashes. Some sheerie dazzle and confuse their victims, leaving them dazed until the morning, or causing them to fall into a deep bog hole. Sheerie are often silent, but some survivors describe hearing a shrieking sound. Others have seen a tiny, wizened face in the light – a truly terrifying sight!

In some parts of Ireland, these lights are called "ghost candles", partly because they can lead people to their end, but also because they have been known to appear in graveyards or other places as a warning of impending death. Sheerie can also appear to guard ancient treasure or as a perilous punishment for some wrongdoing. Some believe sheerie are the souls of ancient ghosts.

Over fourteen per cent of Irish land is covered in bog (though it used to be much more), so it's no surprise to discover that these boglands are also home to faerie folk. Today, Ireland has sixty per cent of Europe's bogs – these malevolent sprites are clearly doing a fierce job protecting them. Many bodies have been discovered in Irish bogs, dating as far back as 2000 BCE. Are these ancient bog bodies the result of these spiteful sprites? Who can say?

Whatever you believe, if you spot lights on the bog, lie down, shut your eyes and don't move if you don't want to end your days in a bog hole. The sheerie will fly off in hunt of another victim or simply vanish into thin air.

> *The usual explanation for these lights is a natural phenomenon created by organic decay.*
>
> *Sheerie are sometimes called Jack o' Lanterns (or Liam na Lasóige), which are believed to be the ghosts of men left to wander lonely places in search of rest, with only a candle in a turnip to light their way.*
>
> *In some parts of Ireland, sheerie are referred to as water goblins and described as tiny, wizened men with long grey beards.*

A Trick of the Light

The minute Liam stepped outside, he knew it was too late: too late to leave his aunt's wake, too late to be returning home and much too late to have accepted the last drink. The taste of it was still in his mouth, making his stomach turn. The walk home would take an eternity. Liam felt dizzy and disorientated. He sat down and plotted his route back. If he crossed the bog before the crossroads, it would take a few minutes off his trip – and even if it was pitch black, it was worth it.

The drizzle was setting in and he started to go over the evening's events. He regretted arguing with his uncle and teasing his cousin. No good would come of it. He looked up and picked himself up from the road.

A light in the distance caught his eye. Liam stood up straight and looked around. *Was it a shooting star?* he wondered. But there weren't any stars out tonight.

The light flashed again, but this time it was pale green instead of a yellowish white. It hovered like a candle, far across the bog. Then another light appeared beside it, flickering. *It must be other guests from the wake.* "Wait! I'll join you," Liam cried.

The bog felt soft underfoot as he plodded heavily across it. The lights flickered. *Don't go out*, he thought, increasing his pace. The lights continued to move ahead, flickering and getting brighter. He peered to see who might be holding them, but he couldn't make out anything, not even a hand.

That's when he heard it: a high-pitched, shrill sound. It was persistent and seemed to be all around him but also inside his head, drumming behind his eyes, between his ears and at the base of his skull.

He had turned back the way he had come when an overwhelming sense of fear gripped him. Liam started to run, but stumbled and picked himself up. The lights were getting bigger and seemed to be moving towards him. The screeching sound intensified.

"Poachers, thieves, ne'er-do-wells," he whispered. "Out to get me."

He saw the lights rise up. *Now I must be dreaming*, he thought when he swore blind he spied tiny, wizened old faces in the lights. One had its mouth open wide, showing tiny, sharp teeth. He dropped to the ground, face down in the peaty, marshy water. He lay still, his eyes shut, frozen in fear. The lights hovered over him. He felt a heavy weight press down on him, pushing him further into the bog – a weight like a mule sitting on him.

Suddenly, the shrill sound became distant. When he looked up, he saw the lights were moving towards the road, as though they were dancing to a jig, keeping time. The weight lifted off him. Liam was shaking so much it took him a few moments to pull himself up. He spent hours walking in circles before collapsing and falling asleep where he lay. He awoke at dawn, still in the bog.

He returned to the village, soaked, stiff and feverish. His hair had turned brilliant white overnight. When he eventually found the courage to tell his story, the old people nodded and sighed. "'Tis the sheerie you encountered. Or some folk in the next parish might tell you it was the Jack o' Lantern or Will the blacksmith wandering the land, looking for his resting place. Whatever it was, you had a lucky escape."

Liam never again set foot on the bog.

GLOSSARY

Ancestor: a person in your family line in the past

BCE: before the Common Era/Christian Era; before the period dating from the birth of Jesus Christ

Bealtaine: an ancient Celtic festival celebrating summer

Beguile: charm or enchant

Bewitch: cast a spell on someone or enchant and delight

CE: Common Era/Christian Era; the period dating from the birth of Jesus Christ, the era we live in

Fae: an old spelling of "faerie"

Lughnasa: an ancient Celtic festival celebrating autumn

Luminous: bright or shining, especially in the dark

Malevolent: wishing evil to others

Megalithic: referring to/describing a stone or stones from the Megalithic Period (2500 BCE – 200 BCE)

Mourner: a person who attends the funeral as a relative or a friend of the dead person

Peril: a situation of immediate danger

Phenomenon: a fact or situation that is observed to exist or happen, especially one whose explanation is in question

Phoenicia: an ancient civilization in the eastern Mediterranean (in modern-day Lebanon)

Psychic: having an ability to predict what will happen in the future

Revere: admire or respect

Samhain: an ancient Celtic festival celebrating winter

Supernatural: a situation or event that is not able to be explained by scientific understanding or the laws of nature

Terrain: an area or type of land

Treacherous: (of land) having hidden or unpredictable dangers

SOURCES

The Schools' Collection, © National Folklore Collection (NFC), UCD, duchas.ie; Angela Bourke, "Economic Necessity and Escapist Fantasy in Éamon a Búrc's Sea-Stories", in Island and Water Dwellers, Four Courts Press, 1999; Caoilte Breatnach, Memories of Time: Folklore of Beithe 1800-2000, Beagh Integrated Rural Development Association, 2003; Katharine Briggs, A Dictionary of Fairies: Hobgoblins, Brownies, Bogies and Other Supernatural Creatures, Allen Lane, 1976; Bob Curran, A Field Guide to Irish Fairies illustrated by Andrew Wilson, Appletree Press, 2007; Colm Duggan, Treasures of Irish Folklore, Mercantile Marketing Consultants Ltd, 1983; Christina Hole, British Folk Customs, Book Club Associates, 1976; W. B. Yeats, Fairy and Folk Tales of Ireland, Colin Smyth, 1973; Eddie Lenihan and Carolyn Eve Green, Meeting the Other Crowd: The Fairy Stories of Hidden Ireland, Gill and MacMillan, 2003; Mark Joyce, Mythical Irish Beasts, Currach Press, 2018; Mark Joyce, Mythical Irish Wonders, Currach Press, 2020; Patricia Lysaght, The Banshee: The Irish Supernatural Death Messenger, The O'Brien Press, 1996; Manchán Magan, Thirty-Two Words for Field: Lost Words of the Irish Landscape, Gill Books, 2022; Marian McGarry, Irish Customs and Rituals: How Our Ancestors Celebrated Life and the Seasons, Orpen Press, 2020; Anne O'Connor, The Blessed and the Damned, Sinful Women and Unbaptised Children in Irish Folklore, Peter Lang, 2005; Dáithí Ó hÓgáin, The Lore of Ireland, An Encyclopaedia of Myth, Legend and Romance, The Collins Press, 2006; Seán Ó Súilleabháin, A Handbook of Irish Folklore, Singing Tree Press, 1970; Seán Ó Súilleabháin, Irish Custom and Belief, Mercer Press, 1977; Diane Perkiss, Troublesome Things: A History of Fairies and Fairy Stories, Penguin, 2000; Nigel Suckling, Faeries of the Celtic Lands, AAPPL, 2007; J. M. Synge, J. M. Synge's The Aran Islands & Connemara, Mercier Press, 2008; Carolyn White, A History of Irish Fairies, Mercier Press, 2008; W. R. Wilde, Irish Popular Superstitions, James McGlashan, 1852

ACKNOWLEDGEMENTS

Thanks to the Arts Council of Ireland for funding my research for this book. The Irish Folklore Collection, especially Ailbe van der Heide. I would like to acknowledge the support from many people in the following organizations: Children's Books Ireland, Books Ireland, Beehive Books, Cubicle 7, Eriu, Gill Books, Irish Academic Press, Little Island, Merrion Press, New Island, The O'Brien Press, Publishing Ireland, Trinity Access Programmes and Veritas. Thanks to Patricia Forde and Ellen Ryan for their endorsements. At Walker, the imitable Gráinne Clear, Isobel Boston, Jamie Hammond and Conor Hackett. A massive thank you to Dermot Flynn for his magical illustrations and for getting my stories straight away. Thanks to Gráinne Mhaol Ní Máille for checking the Irish spellings.

Orla Brennan, Ciara Elliott, Willow Burke, Quentin Fottrell, Mick Quinlan, Emma Burke-Kennedy, Ruth Burke-Kennedy, Ally Mundie, Carla Brooks, Tara O'Reilly, Karen Kavanagh, Fiona Brennan, Fiona Lennon, Catherine Ann Cullen, Catherine Heaney, Margaret Anne Suggs, Joby Hickey, Susan O'Loghlin, Tinky Freeman, Amanda Bell, Helen Carr, Emma Byrne, the Cohort and the Beynackers, and all my dear friends, you know who you are.

To my dad, Ruairí, who passed on his love of storytelling. To my late mother, Nicola, whose love and support remain. My brothers: Malachi, for reminding me not to tell tales, and Conan, for insisting I tell him stories from my "mind". A massive thanks to my family at home: Martin, Daniel and Benjamin Bradley, for their encouragement and unwavering support. To Poppy, for fetching me back when I was away with the faeries.

First published 2024 by Walker Books Ltd, 87 Vauxhall Walk, London SE11 5HJ • Text © 2024 Síne Quinn • Illustrations © 2024 Dermot Flynn • The right of Síne Quinn and Dermot Flynn to be identified as author and illustrator respectively of this work has been asserted in accordance with the Copyright, Designs and Patents Act 1988 • This book has been typeset in Joanna MT and Modern Antiqua • Printed in China • All rights reserved. No part of this book may be reproduced, transmitted or stored in an information retrieval system in any form or by any means, graphic, electronic or mechanical, including photocopying, taping and recording, without prior written permission from the publisher. British Library Cataloguing in Publication Data: a catalogue record for this book is available from the British Library • ISBN 978-1-5295-1860-3 • www.walker.co.uk • EU Authorized Representative: HackettFlynn Ltd, 36 Cloch Choirneal, Balrothery, Co. Dublin, K32 C942, Ireland. EU@walkerpublishinggroup.com • 10 9 8 7 6 5 4 3 • The author received financial support from the Arts Council of Ireland in the creation of this work